FESTIVALS

MYRA COHN LIVINGSTON, POET

LEONARD EVERETT FISHER, PAINTER

Holiday House / New York

Printed in the United States of America
First Edition
Library of Congress Cataloging-in-Publication Data
Livingston, Myra Cohn.
    Festivals / Myra Cohn Livingston, Poet ; Leonard Everett Fisher,
  painter.—1st ed.
        p.   cm.
    Summary: Poems celebrating fourteen festivals observed around the
world including Chinese New Year, Kwanzaa, Purim, and Tet-Nguyen
-dan.
    ISBN 0-8234-1217-2 (hardcover : alk. paper)
    1. Festivals—Juvenile poetry. 2. Children's poetry, American.
  [1. Festivals—Poetry. 2. American poetry.] I. Fisher, Leonard
Everett, ill. II. Title.
PS3562.I945F47   1996   95-31055   CIP   AC
811'.54—dc20

CONTENTS

CHINESE NEW YEAR

Flowers and *Nin Wah*,
Tangerines, oranges,
Wealth and good fortune
    and luck to us all!

Midnight will bring us
Red envelopes, *Lai-See*,
Filled with some money
    and riches for all!

Time for remembering
Grandparents, parents,
Neighbors and friends:
    with fine gifts for them all!

We will be offered
A tray of togetherness,
Seeds, candied coconut,
    sweetmeats for all!

Days of the Dragon Play,
Nights filled with singing,
Then comes *Ten Chieh*
    with lanterns for all!

Soon the parade starts—
With loud firecrackers!—
The dragon is here!—
    Happy New Year to all!

TET NGUYEN-DAN

Great-grandma says
a New Year prayer
as she remembers
when and where

she lived her days
in Vietnam,
and how the festival
began;

bright altars filled
with fruits and flowers,
incense and music;
all the hours

she learned to give
and to forgive,
to eat *banh day*,
to laugh and live.

She tells us that
a *palaquin*
helps us to know
what life can mean,

for anyone
up in that chair
has studied hard
to sit up there,

reminding us
we, too, can rise,
that education
makes us wise—

so when we celebrate
on TET,
Great-grandma says
not to forget

to work and study,
dance and sing,
watch fireworks,
and welcome Spring!

MARDI GRAS

Throw me
something, Mister,
I shout to the krewes on
their floats, rolling down Bourbon Street.
Throw me

something
from behind your
mask, a string of glass beads,
purple beads for justice, beads of green
for faith,

doubloons
of bright gold for
power. *Throw me something*
now that it's Fat Tuesday and it's
time for

music,
dancing, singing,
and you, *Mister*, on your
float reaching for something you can
throw me—

10

PURIM

I will
stamp on his name!
Mordechai would not bow
before him so in anger he
plotted

to kill
the Jews, until
Esther came to tell the truth
to King Ahasverosh. This meant
the Jews

were spared,
and he was hanged!
Then everyone was as
happy as we are on Purim
when we

hear the
ancient story——
yelling, screaming, stamping our
feet, shaking the *groggers* at the
name of

Haman,
the evil one,
reminding us that this
one day we stamp out hatred with
laughter!

CHERRY BLOSSOM FESTIVAL

What do they hide in
their giant fists, these fragrant,
pink, cherry blossoms?

NOW-RUZ

All of
us jump across
the bonfire, asking for
good fortune, good luck and many
blessings;

all of
us wear new clothes,
get gifts of coins, and eat
a whole batch of sweet *baklava*
until

all of
us have to go
outdoors on the thirteenth
day when it isn't lucky for us
to stay

indoors,
so Father can
throw wheat sprouts into the
the river like he's throwing away
family

quarrels,
so all of us
can start off a happy
New Year in peace and harmony
again.

ARBOR DAY

Into earth
I dig
dark space
where
roots
may grow
and from
this
place
a trunk
will rise,
Spring branches
spread
over the earth,
and Fall boughs
shed
bright colored leaves:

All this will be
forever—
when I
plant a tree.

RAMADAN AND ID-UL-FITR

I get hungry.
I don't mind.

Ramadan's a
special time
to fast all day
to think of when
Mohammed lived,
and how again
we fill our souls
in every way,
our spirits quiet
as we pray:
Our month to learn,
to understand
what Islam means
in every land.

Each night
we break
our daily fast,
but Id-Ul-Fitr
comes at last:
The fast is over!
There are treats—
new clothes, and coins,
delicious sweets,
and at the fair
we get to see
magicians,
jugglers,
revelry
and music—
It's a happy time.

I get hungry.
I don't mind.

CREEK INDIAN BUSK OR NEW YEAR: THE OLD MEN'S DANCE

When pokeweed berries ripened,
when leaves turned
red and gold,
the young men danced The Old Men's Dance.
like Indians of old.

With pumpkin, gourd, or melon
they made strange masks to wear.
They fastened dangling earrings
and sumac stalks
for hair.

Two slitted holes were carved
for eyes.
The one big hole beneath
was shaped exactly like a mouth
with grains of corn for teeth.

And then
from pokewood berries
each mask, each cunning face
was stained with deepest purple,
and with their shawls in place

they fastened
noisy rattles
made out of tortoise shell
around their legs, and then began
to weave a wondrous spell:

With painted purple faces
and wigs of sumac hair,
with corn teeth, hollow rattles
shaking
through autumn air,

as though
they were young hunters
of vigor, strength and skill,
they arched their bows and arrows
to dance the hunt, the kill.

The Old Men's Dance is over.
The last who saw are gone,
Yet still the old men's spirit
keeps dancing—
dancing on.

DIWALI

On the wings
of the Heavenly Swan
she rides
down to
our
golden lights

strung on the windows
and houses
and roofs
on this,
the most wondrous
of nights,

when
the *dipas*
are glowing,
the flowers festooned,
and we wait
for the moments
to fly

when Lakshmi
returns
with good fortune,
and
fireworks
splash
in the
sky!

EL DÍA DE MUERTOS:
THE DAY OF THE DEAD

On our
ofrenda we
place pictures, clothes, food, masks,
and *calaveras;* whatever
they loved

in life
is here, waiting
for them, and we carry
baskets of food, and flowers from
our house

making
a golden path
of fragrant marigolds,
sprinkling the petals by handfuls
along

the road
from our doorstep
to the far cemetery
so the spirits may find their way
back home.

THE FEAST OF ST. LUCY: LUCIADAGEN

And I will stay awake throughout the longest winter night
And dress up in a red silk sash and flowing gown of white
And serve my parents with warm sweets and sing for their delight.

And I will wear upon my head a crown of fragrant green
Ablaze with tall white candles, with golden candle-gleam,
And I will be a *Lussibrud* as in some wondrous dream.

And as the night begins to fade I'll greet December sun
And knock on all the neighbors' doors and sing to everyone
And offer all the friends I greet a golden saffron bun.

Lucia maidens will come too, with silver in their hair
And star boys with their studded wands and pointed caps to wear,
And elfin boys will follow us as we walk everywhere.

And I will stay awake throughout the longest winter night
And dress up in my silken sash, my crown, my robe of white
And I will be, for one brief day, Lucia of the Light.

26

LAS POSADAS: (THE INNS)

The First Night

Who walks through dusk and firelight?
Who knocks upon our door tonight?

A pilgrim, traveling this way,
Seeks out a room, a place to stay.

I do not know your name, your kin.
There is no room within this inn.

The Second Night

The night is dark. My wife is weak.
A restful bed is all we seek.

I cannot tell your origin
No strangers tarry at this inn.

The Third Night

We come this hour from Galilee
To pay our taxes by decree.

I never let a traveler in
Unknown to me. Not at this inn.

The Fourth Night

We seek not much, a crust of bread—
A spot to lay a weary head.

You look like beggars, weary, thin.
My guests are wealthy at this inn.

The Fifth Night

I ask for shelter for my wife;
Within her lives another life.

I fear she could not bear the din.
We've merrymakers at this inn.

The Sixth Night

For days we've traveled on the road.
Our spirits bear a heavy load.

> *It matters not where you have been.*
> *I take no strangers at this inn.*

The Seventh Night

A bed for her—a crust for one—
She will not trouble anyone.

> *I have no bed or food herein*
> *There is no shelter at this inn.*

The Eighth Night

My fear is great, my heart is wild
For her who bears an unborn child.

> *My guests are all asleep within.*
> *Our rooms are taken at this inn.*

The Ninth Night

> *Who walks through dusk and firelight?*
> *Who knocks upon the door this night?*

A pilgrim knocks. The night is drear,
And Mary, Queen of Heaven, here—

> *Then welcome friends and enter in!*
> *There's room for all within this inn!*

This poem can be presented as a play, with Mary and Joseph and the nine innkeepers, as well as those who are guests at the inn, and those who come with the procession to watch them as they go from inn to inn.

KWANZAA

*Where there is Kwanzaa
    there is corn:*

An ear of corn
for every child;

Where there is corn
there is a dream,

a dream of growth
wondrous and wild;

a dream of strength,
of unity

for generations
yet unborn.

Where there is dreaming
there is child.

*Where there is Kwanzaa
    there is corn.*

GLOSSARY

Arbor Day: This day is celebrated in various parts of the United States at different times, often falling on the fourth Friday in April. The first Arbor Day took place on April 10, 1871, when the people of Nebraska planted more than one million trees. A similar holiday, *Tu B'Shvat*, was begun in Israel in 1948.

Cherry Blossom Festival: From ancient times cherry blossoms have been a symbol for simplicity, beauty, and purity. Each spring, when the cherry trees are in bloom, the Japanese follow news of the *sakura zensen* or "cherry blossom blooming front" as the trees bloom from south to north. There are cherry-blossom dances in Kyoto and parties all over Japan during which people view the trees. In Washington, D.C., where cherry trees, a gift from the Japanese, were planted in 1912, there is a Cherry Blossom Festival each spring.

Chinese New Year (January 20–February 19): Beginning at midnight on New Year's Eve, people seal their doors and stay up late in hopes it will mean a longer life for the parents. Houses are cleaned, no bad language is allowed, and everyone is encouraged to repay their debts before the old year dies. Firecrackers are set off to attract the attention of the gods and scare off evil spirits. There is singing, the eating of special foods, and social visits. *Nin Wah* are pictures, *Lai-See* is good luck money. *Ten Chieh*, the Feast of the Lanterns, and a parade end the festival.

Creek Indian Busk or New Year: The Old Men's Dance (September–October): This is the last of two dances performed by the Creek Indians to celebrate the harvest. It is one of many Native American dances that celebrate the corn harvest.

Diwali (October–November): Sometimes known as Divali or Dewali (Hindu Festival of Lights), this is a week-long celebration marking the beginning of the Hindu year. *Dipas*, oil-burning lamps that children make from clay saucers and mustard oil, are placed on rooftops, garden paths, balconies, and window ledges. A thousand lights might be lit in one house alone. *Lakshmi* is the Hindu goddess of fortune and wealth who may appear riding on the wings of a heavenly swan. She is supposed to bring wealth and good luck to the people if they wear their finest clothes, keep their houses clean, and welcome her with wreaths of flowers in their doorways. Another story connected to this holiday is about *Shri Ram*, a god who returns to his kingdom after defeating the evil dragon *Ravana*.

El Día de Muertos: The Day of The Dead: On November 1 and 2, families remember those who have died. In their homes, they erect an *ofrenda*, or altar, decorated with an arch of flowers, *calaveras* (skulls of white sugar), photographs, pictures, masks, favorite foods, possessions, and offerings to their loved ones. Families also visit the cemetery, picnic there, and decorate the gravesites with golden marigolds in memory of the adults. White flowers are for departed children.

Kwanzaa (meaning "first fruits" in Swahili) starts on December 26 and lasts for seven days. Created in 1966 by Maulana Karenga, an African-American professor at the University of California, it celebrates the connection between African-Americans and their African past, as well as the strength of the African-American community. It includes the *Nguzo Saba*, seven symbols and seven principles: *Umoja*, unity; *Kujichagulia*, self-determination; *Ujima*, collective work and responsibility; *Ujamaa*, cooperative economics; *Nia*, purpose; *Kuumba*, creativity and beauty; and *Imani*, faith. There is a special candlelighting ceremony, *Mishumaa saba*, and a celebration of the first harvest of African crops.

Las Posadas: (The Inns) (December 16–24):   A *posada* is an inn or lodging place. *Las Posadas* represents Mary and Joseph's journey as they searched for lodging in Bethlehem before the birth of Jesus. Often children act out the couple's search, carrying statues of Mary and Joseph on *andas*, tall sticks, as they lead a procession to nine different houses.

The Feast of St. Lucy: Luciadagen (December 13):   On December 13 the eldest daughter in the family plays the part of *Lussibrud*, the Lucia bride, dressing in a long white robe tied with a bright red sash. On her head is a wreath of evergreens and lighted candles. She offers *lussekatter*, Lucia cats, twisted saffron buns in the shape of an X, with eyes made of raisins. Saint Lucy is a legendary figure. Born in Sicily of wealthy Christians, she gave away her riches to the poor and was later put to death by the Romans. Her name in Latin, *Lux*, means "light."

Mardi Gras: Held on Shrove or Fat Tuesday 41 days before Easter, it is the last day of feasting and celebration before Lent begins. In New Orleans, Louisiana, Mardi Gras is a special holiday with parades, balls, costumes, and masks. *Krewes*, the private clubs and organizations that put on the parade, ride the floats dressed in costumes, throwing gifts and beads to the crowds that line the streets. Mardi Gras is a legal holiday in Louisiana but is also celebrated in Alabama, Texas, and Florida, and several countries outside the United States.

Now-Ruz: Beginning on March 21, Now-Ruz is a celebration of the Iranian New Year. There is a special feast with seven foods, beginning with the letter S. Each represents one of the seven spiritual forces of religious practices that date back to before Islam. The events include jumping over a bonfire, dancing, music, a special meal, and the custom of going outdoors on the thirteenth day, as it is considered unlucky to stay inside. At this time, the father performs the ritual of throwing wheat which he has grown for two weeks, into the river. *Baklava* is a dessert made from honey, nuts, and thin shells of pastry.

Purim (February–March):   A Jewish holiday, it is sometimes called the Feast of Queen Esther. Haman, minister to King Ahasverosh, was angry at the Jews because Esther's uncle, Mordechai, would not bow down to him. Haman persuaded the king to order all Jews to be destroyed. When Queen Esther pleaded with her husband to save her people, the king did as she asked. *Groggers* are noisemakers that children shake to drown out Haman's name when they hear the story. People eat poppyseed and prune-filled cakes called *Hamantashen*, meaning Haman's pockets. Actually they are shaped like Haman's hat and are baked in the shape of triangles.

Ramadan and Id-Ul-Fitr: In the ninth month of the Muslim lunar year, Muslims enjoy Ramadan at the full moon. They do not eat, drink, or smoke from sunrise to sunset until the next full moon. At the end of this period, there is a three day festival known as *Id-Ul-Fitr*. *Id* means happiness and *Fitr* means breaking the Fast. This is a time of joy and prayers when everyone worships at the mosque, enjoys the first noon meal in a month, and attends fairs where there are puppet shows, merry-go-rounds, ferris wheels, and fireworks. On the last day of *Id-Ul-Fitr*, families visit each other and children receive gifts.

Tet Nguyen-Dan (January 21–February 19):   China ruled Vietnam for ten centuries, so this holiday reflects many Chinese customs. Usually known as TET, the most important festival in Vietnam, it is a time for new clothes, clean houses, giving and forgiving, paying off debts, fun, and feasting. *Bahn day* are rice cakes. A *palaquin* is a boxlike chair carried on poles by several men in which someone of importance rides.